For Rachel, very dearly missed — S. R.
For Will, with love — J. J.

Text copyright © 2002 by Shen Roddie
Illustrations copyright © 2002 by Jenny Jones

Published by Bloomsbury, New York and London
Distributed to the trade by St. Martin's Press

Library of Congress Cataloging-in-Publication Data
Roddie, Shen. Sandbear / by Shen Roddie ; illustrated by Jenny
Jones. p. cm. Summary: After Hare makes a sandbear out of sand, he
and his new friend discover the importance of giving. [1.
Friendship—Fiction 2. Hares—Fiction 3. Bear—Fiction] 1. Title.
PZ7.R5998 San 2002 [E]—dc-21 2001043977
ISBN: 1-58234-758-1

First U.S. Edition 2002
10 9 8 7 6 5 4 3 2 1

Bloomsbury USA Children's Books
175 Fifth Avenue
New York, New York 10010

SANDBEAR

by Shen Roddie

illustrated by Jenny Jones

BLOOMSBURY
CHILDREN'S
BOOKS

Out in the dunes, a wild wind blew and the sands shivered. It made quivery sand waves and puffy little sandhills.

"I can see a Sandbear in here!" said Hare, looking at a little sand mound. Hare dug some sand and flung it at the sandhill. He sloshed some water from his bucket to wet it.

"There!" he said. "You'll make a perfect Sandbear!"

A body's no good without a head, thought Hare. So he tossed some sand over Sandbear's body.

"A funny-looking head but what great ears! You won't mind, will you, Bear?" laughed Hare.

"As for your eyes, these little pebbles will do," said Hare as he put them on Sandbear's face.

"They're all I can find in a hurry!"

"A bear needs a sniffer!" said Hare, plonking a nose-sized piece of driftwood where a bear's nose should be.

"It's not a bear's nose I know, but you'll get used to it!"

"Just one more thing!" said Hare as he jabbed a finger under bear's nose.

"A pinhole mouth!" laughed Hare.

Then Hare traced out two short legs.
"That'll do for a bear who's not going
anywhere!" he said.

Hare stood back to take a look.
"You look just like a friend!" he cried.
"We could picnic together, you and I.
But you'll need hands for that."

Hare grabbed a handful of sand.
Then he let go of it.

"It will take forever to make a pair
of hands," he groaned. "I need something
quick and easy!"

"I know!" said Hare, shoving a blade of grass into Sandbear's side. "A friendly one-armed bandit."

"I'd love to make you handsomer but it's hard work and I don't have all day," said Hare. "I've got to go; it's munchtime! See you tomorrow if the wild winds don't blow. Bye, Sandbear!"

And Hare hopped away.

Not long after, the wild winds did blow.

"Brrrr … I'm cold," said Sandbear, brushing sand from his eye. "I wish I had a coat to keep me warm."

Sandbear tried to gallop quickly to the woods.

Clop! Clop!

Sandbear thought the woods would keep him warm.

But Sandbear could not gallop
quickly. His legs were too short.
So he shuffled slowly to the woods
where he could be warm.

Sandbear shuffled a long, long way.

He stumbled across a sandcrab.

He stepped on a green frog.

"That's my tail you're treading on, Sandbear!" said a field mouse.
"Oops, sorry!" said Sandbear.

If only I had big, bright eyes, he thought.

Sandbear was hungry. He found a carrot but could not pull it out. His grass hand was no good. So he dug at it with his nose and out it popped.

"*Yum!*" said Sandbear. He tried to eat it, but his mouth was too small.
"Silly Hare!" he said.

Just then, he heard a cry.
"Help! Somebody help!"

Sandbear shuffled toward the voice
as fast as he could.
"Where are you?" he called.
"Here!" wailed the voice.

It seems to be coming from here, thought Sandbear. Sandbear looked down a deep, dark hole.

"I see two floppy ears!" he cried. "It's Hare!"

Hare had fallen into a deep pit. He was shaking with fear.

"Whistle a happy tune, Hare, while I get you out," said Sandbear.

"How will you get me out?" asked Hare.

"By doing my very best!" said Sandbear.

Sandbear looked around for a rope but there wasn't one.

He leaned over. "Here! Hold on to my hand and don't let go," said Sandbear and he lowered his grass hand as far down as he could.

"Have you got it, friend?" asked Sandbear.

"Yes!" replied Hare but as soon as he said that, Sandbear lost his hand!

Hare had pulled it off!

"Oh no!" cried Hare.
"Oh no!" sighed Sandbear.

Then Sandbear said, "I'm coming!" and he slid down, down, down the deep, dark hole.

"Hare!" cried Sandbear as he disappeared into the darkness. "Hop out quick!"

Hare leaped on top of Sandbear and jumped out. "Thanks, Sandbear!" said Hare, peering into the pit. "You've saved my life!"

But all Hare saw was a pile of sand with two little pebbles, a piece of driftwood and a blade of grass.

There was no Sandbear.
Sandbear was no more!

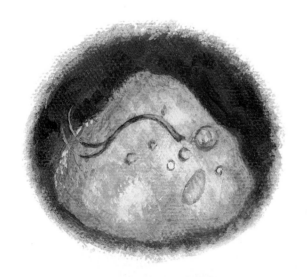

"Sandbear! Oh, Sandbear!" cried Hare, a big tear bursting down his cheek. "You're in there! I know you are! I'll get you out! You'll see!"

Hare grabbed a spade. Then carefully, very carefully, Hare dug Sandbear out.

He piled him high. Carefully, very carefully, he drizzled water over the sand. He patted a shape. A shape with two strong legs.

Then he made a head.
A familiar, peculiar Sandbear head.

Hare shaped two strong arms for Sandbear's hugs.

Then he hunted for a pair of shiny, black pebbles.

"There, bright eyes!" said Hare.

Hare put Sandbear's nose back on. "So I will always know it's you!"

And to stop him from freezing when the wild winds blew, Hare lent Sandbear his hat and vest. "I haven't forgotten your mouth, Sandbear. How would you like it, my dear friend?" asked Hare.

Sandbear s-t-r-e-t-c-h-ed out his arms. "BIG!"

"I thought so!" said Hare. "Perfect for a bear dinner!"

At the word "dinner," Sandbear picked Hare
up with his big bear arms. He swung him
high in the air. Then dropped him—*plop!*—
onto his big bear shoulders.

"Come on, my friend," said Sandbear.
"Off to the woods we go. It's picnic time!"

And with the wild wind behind them,
they vanished into the woods ahead.